On this date

_____

a **Magical Mermaid**

arrived in the Wonder Window to help

_____

(Name)

find the gifts of the sea, the treasures on earth,

and the magic of life.

Illustrated by Martha-Elizabeth Ferguson.

ISBN: 0-9634910-9-1

Library of Congress Card Number: 2001088276

10 9 8 7 6 5 4 3 2 1 First Edition March 2002

Printed in China

My Magical Mermaid

Samara Anjelae

To George Sourati,

a kind merman who lives by the sea

BelleTress Books

From the earliest Greek tales to present day accounts, mermaids have appeared in literature, art, and in sightings by fishermen and sea people all over the world. Mermaids are the mysterious ocean goddesses and gods that protect the sea and the sea animals. They live in and beneath the waters. Mermaids are known for having the ability to change their shimmery tails into human legs when they desire to walk upon dry land. No matter how long they stay on land, they are always said to be drawn back to the sea.

Mermaids warn birds of approaching storms, untangle octopuses, corral sea horses, and free playful sea pups caught in kelp beds. They are also known for their voices—a wonderful sweetness that can distract the best of seafarers. Mermaids sometimes annoy fishermen by removing the bait from the hooks to keep their fish friends from harm. Yet, in stormy weather they help fishermen arrive home safely. These ocean creatures make frequent trips ashore, if only to sit on a rock and comb out their long hair.

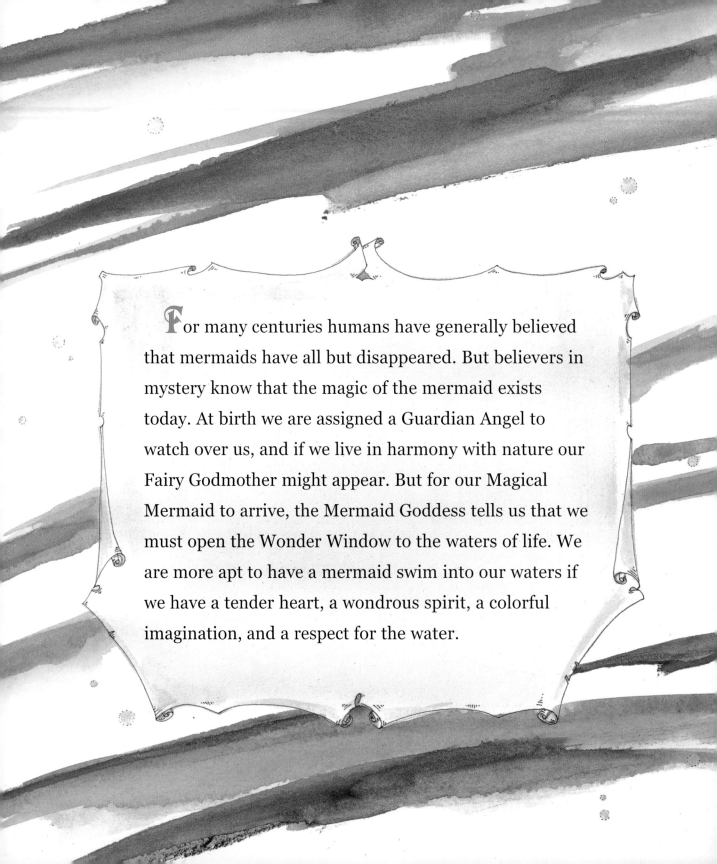

For many centuries humans have generally believed that mermaids have all but disappeared. But believers in mystery know that the magic of the mermaid exists today. At birth we are assigned a Guardian Angel to watch over us, and if we live in harmony with nature our Fairy Godmother might appear. But for our Magical Mermaid to arrive, the Mermaid Goddess tells us that we must open the Wonder Window to the waters of life. We are more apt to have a mermaid swim into our waters if we have a tender heart, a wondrous spirit, a colorful imagination, and a respect for the water.

While mermaids are faithful to the sea, they also have the desire to aid humans. Mermaids have many unusual powers. They can remind us that we are a part of nature and link us to the ocean of love. Mermaids can foretell events. They are able to predict storms at sea and trouble on land. They can also inspire humans to shine with color and create magic in their lives. Use your imagination to meet your Magical Mermaid. Imagine everything you can about your mermaid, then swim down through the waters to this magical realm.

The water covering seventy percent of the earth has always mesmerized humans. Without water there would be no life on land. Scientists and oceanographers have accomplished much in their study of marine life, yet they have not reached the depths of the sea. Mermaids live throughout the oceans in many colors, shapes and sizes. These Water Dancers live at the bottom of the seas in their many palaces and villages. In the Treasury of Mermaid Lore it is said that mermaids have love in their hearts, healing in their hands, talent in their tails and magic in their thoughts.

Dolphins are known as messengers between the mermaid world and the human world. If you spot one dancing and playing in the ocean, then know a mermaid might be near. Dolphins love to play, help and heal humans. Dolphins may visit mermaid villages, but they always emerge from their underwater travel to breathe and share their experiences. They inspire humans to be in a playful state, where our mood is light and our happiness shows. You can imitate the dolphin and discover the flow of breath by riding the waves of laughter and spreading joyful play and creativity.

The Magical Mermaid Alphabet

M is for Making a wish to your Mermaid.

A is for Admiring the beauty of the seas.

G is for Greeting your mermaid with a Grin.

I is for Igniting your Imagination with creativity.

C is for Caring for the water and the water babies.

A is for Anticipating your magical encounter.

L is for Living with splashes of color and fun.

 is for Manifesting Miracles on land and sea.

 is for Encouraging others to see with festive eyes.

 is for Remembering the impossible is possible.

 is for Moonbathing with your shimmery friend.

 is for Awakening the land under the waves.

 is for Including others in your delightful discovery.

 is for Dancing through life with your

Magical Mermaid!

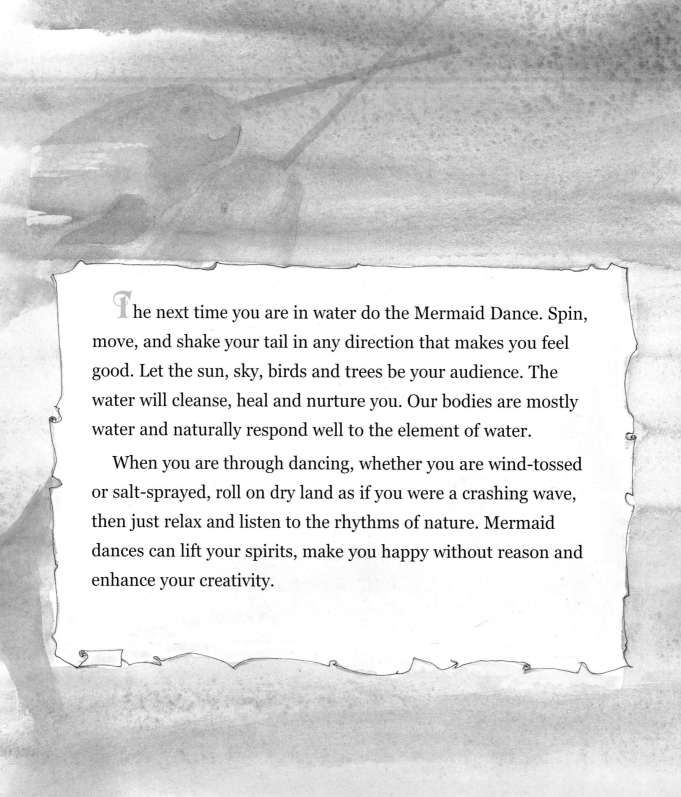

The next time you are in water do the Mermaid Dance. Spin, move, and shake your tail in any direction that makes you feel good. Let the sun, sky, birds and trees be your audience. The water will cleanse, heal and nurture you. Our bodies are mostly water and naturally respond well to the element of water.

When you are through dancing, whether you are wind-tossed or salt-sprayed, roll on dry land as if you were a crashing wave, then just relax and listen to the rhythms of nature. Mermaid dances can lift your spirits, make you happy without reason and enhance your creativity.

Have you traveled to other parts of the world? Our oceans bring the world together with the many shorelines that join different cultures and communities. Turn the page and explore the world map. Let the mermaids of the four great oceans take you on a journey.

The *Indian Sea Queen* is the guardian of the water from southern Asia to Antarctica and from eastern Africa to southwest Australia. The *Pacific Sea Queen* rules the largest of the world's oceans, extending from the western Americas to eastern Asia and Australia. The *Arctic Sea Queen* lives in the waters surrounding the North Pole. The *Atlantic Sea Queen* travels between the Arctic in the north to the Antarctic in the south between the eastern Americas and western Europe and Asia.

THE
INDIAN AND PACIFIC
SEA QUEEN

ARCTIC OCEAN

GREENLAND

EUROPE

ARCTIC
AND THE ATLANTIC
SEA QUEEN

NORTH AMERICA

CARIBBEAN SEA

AFRICA

ATLANTIC OCEAN

SOUTH AMERICA

Friends of Mermaids

Traditionally, mermaids are regarded as a good omen.
These magical creature have a kinship with all life.

Sun

Moon

Stars

Fairies

Angels

Dolphins

Fish

Whales

Humans

Seals

Manatees

Starfish

Sea Horses

Sea Turtles

Sand Dollars

The sea people have languages all of their own – the true languages of love – that are never spoken.

The *Beautiful Language* is expressed by singing, chanting, and playing musical instruments such as cymbals, drums, flutes, harps and rain sticks.

The *Blissful Language* consists of kisses, blowing kisses, butterfly kisses, waves by hand or mermaid tails, hugs, grins, ear wiggles, handshakes, winks and double winks.

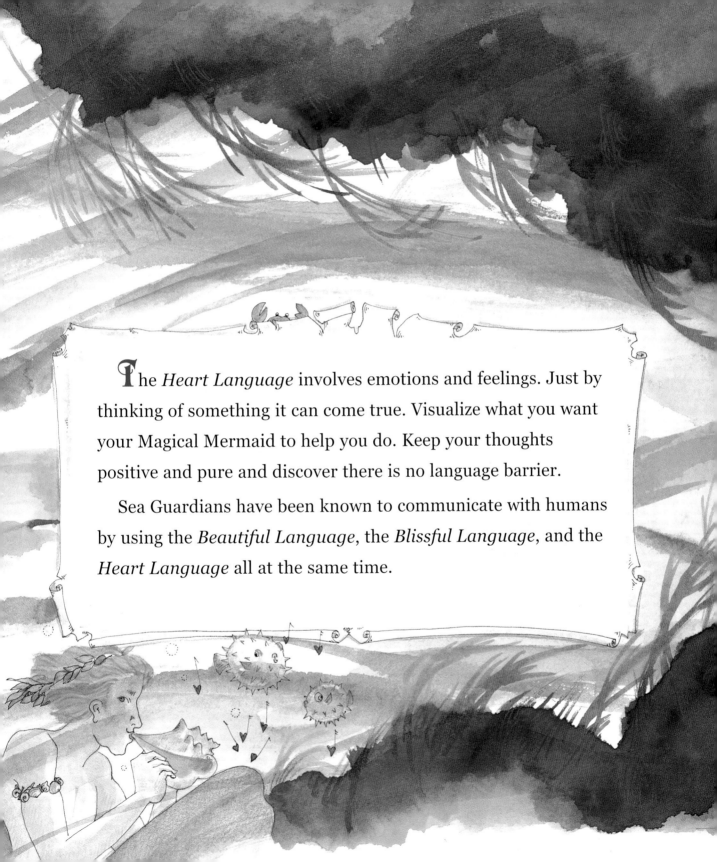

The *Heart Language* involves emotions and feelings. Just by thinking of something it can come true. Visualize what you want your Magical Mermaid to help you do. Keep your thoughts positive and pure and discover there is no language barrier.

Sea Guardians have been known to communicate with humans by using the *Beautiful Language*, the *Blissful Language*, and the *Heart Language* all at the same time.

Mermaids are inspired by the sound of peaceful music. On moonlit nights when most humans are asleep they join the land fairies and the angels to sing, dance and play. Mermaids link the rhythm of music to the rhythm of water. If you are fortunate, you can hear the enchanted tones of the Angelic Choir, the Fairy Carolers and the Mermaid Vocalists. They sing and play the Song of Oneness and rejoice to the blessings of life. They invite animals, children and kind people to join them in their celebration, either through their dreams or with their imaginative minds.

The Moon Lady is mysterious and beautiful. She changes her appearance a little every day and has many phases to her personality. Each time she changes her moonbeam, sparkles shed down on earth. When there is a Full Moon, mermaids make their presence known by leaving many magical gifts, sometimes called being "moonstruck." When there is a Half-Moon, mermaids give respect to those who feel different from others. They know how it is to be unusual since they can be half-human and half-fish at the same time.

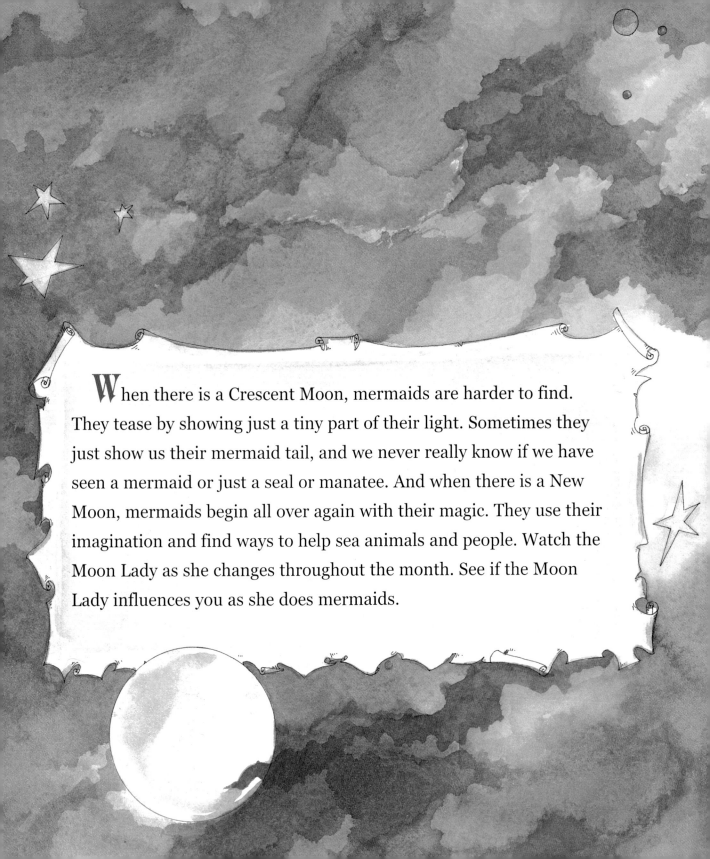

When there is a Crescent Moon, mermaids are harder to find. They tease by showing just a tiny part of their light. Sometimes they just show us their mermaid tail, and we never really know if we have seen a mermaid or just a seal or manatee. And when there is a New Moon, mermaids begin all over again with their magic. They use their imagination and find ways to help sea animals and people. Watch the Moon Lady as she changes throughout the month. See if the Moon Lady influences you as she does mermaids.

Wishing Well Wishes

Throw a special coin into a body of water; a wishing well. It might be a spring, pond, stream, ocean, lake, river, fountain or waterfall. Make two wishes. Create one wish for you and create one for humankind. Asking is a positive step and sets the action in motion. It helps to include in your wish the phrase, "for the highest good of all concerned." When your aspirations have been made, mermaids swim the waters to help make them come true. Close all your requests with an expression of gratitude. Mermaids also have their own requests. Their global wish is that humans will make wise choices about their environment to ensure safe, clean and resourceful waters for today and for future generations.

Mermaid Wishes for You

Wild Hair

Moon Sparkles

Graceful Moves

Scales of Beauty

Splashes of Color

Stars of Compassion

Sweet Singing Voice

Shells of Splendor

Sea of Confidence

Mermaid Wisdom

Dolphin Intuition

Turtle Patience

Sun Smiles

Mermaids have been the subject of curiosity throughout time and have inspired works of music, literature and art. They have been called:

Water Dancers

Sea-Folk

Sky Watchers

Ocean Singers

Water Babies

Merpersons

Sea Guardians

Moon Bathers

Water Watchtowers

Sea Nymphs

Be Like a Mermaid

Watch the Sky

Play in the Sun

Frolic in the Water

Swim with Dolphins

Dance under the Moon

Splash in Rain Puddles

Take Swimming Lessons

Feed Fish and Marine Life

Comb your Hair in the Sun

Whistle in the Shower or Tub

Sing Love Songs to our Creator

Find Rainbow Light in Waterfalls

Shed a Salt Tear When you Need To

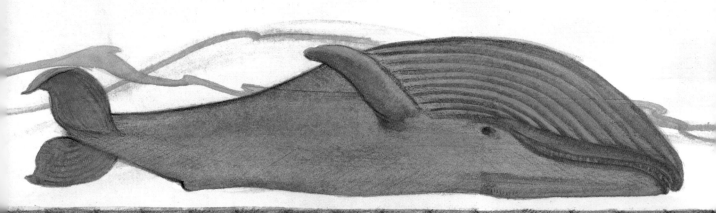

Remember, in every Wonder Window there are sparkling treasures. Keep on believing in yourself, in mermaids, and in the magic of life.

Wonder Window Series

A collection of timeless books that are a treasury of soul wisdom,
making them fine gifts for all ages.

Other books in the Wonder Window Series:

My Guardian Angel, an enchanting book that promotes a deeper understanding of angels and our relationship with our Guardian Angel.

A Guardian Angel is assigned to every soul's Wonder Window for guidance, love and protection throughout the journey of life.

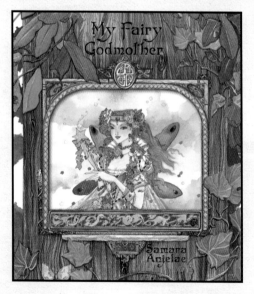

My Fairy Godmother, an entertaining and imaginative book that takes you into the realm of fairies. A Fairy Godmother appears in the Wonder Window to help you discover the beauty, love and spirit in every living creature.

BelleTress Books